INVISIBLE
IN THE THIRD GRADE

Margery Cuyler

INVISIBLE
IN THE THIRD GRADE

illustrated by Mirko Gabler

SCHOLASTIC INC.
New York Toronto London Auckland Sydney

Thanks to Elizabeth Winthrop and Pete Parsells
for their thoughtful comments and to Jan,
Thomas, and Timothy Perkins for their support

ISBN 0-590-92881-3

24 23 22 21 20 19 18 17 16 15 14   1/0

Printed in the U.S.A.   40

First Scholastic printing, September 1996

CONTENTS

INVISIBLE
IN THE THIRD GRADE

· 1 ·
THE MAGIC GUM

Alex Parsells was walking home from the bus stop, thinking about his bad day. First his mother had given him oatmeal for breakfast. "It's healthy," she'd said, "especially with sliced bananas on top." Alex thought that oatmeal and bananas tasted like wet paper with slimy slugs mixed in. But he'd eaten his breakfast anyway, so as not to fight with his mother. Then, while he was waiting for the school bus, it had started to rain. He'd arrived soaking wet in Mrs. DeLarato's third-grade classroom. Finally, Alex's twelve-year-old brother, Pete, was meeting with the Gang after school. Alex had begged Pete a thousand times to let him join the Gang, but Pete had said Alex was too young. "Only sixth graders can be members," he'd told him.

Alex hardly ever saw his brother anymore. Lately the Gang had been taking all of Pete's time. Pete no longer helped Alex with his homework or played soccer with him in the backyard. He was too busy with the Gang.

As Alex walked by the Mobil station on Mercer Street, he stopped to get a package of bubble gum. Chewing gum always made him feel better. That way he could chew up his troubles. When he blew bubbles, he could blow them away.

Alex walked into the office and stood in front of the candy and gum machine. It had his favorite brand, Double Bubble Yummy Gum. He took three quarters from his pocket, pushed them into the coin slot, and pressed the buttons. A package fell into the tray, but it didn't look right. "Hmm," Alex said to himself. "There's something weird about this gum. It glows." Its pink-and-silver paper gave off a soft light as it lay in his palm. Alex squinted to read the label: ZXO'S DOUBLE-TROUBLE BUBBLE GUM. He shrugged and pulled out a stick of gum. He unwrapped it and stuck it in his mouth. It tasted like all the most wonderful things he could imagine blended together. Alex closed his eyes and enjoyed the different flavors—strawberry, marshmallow, raspberry, and a hint of licorice.

6 • Invisible in the Third Grade

On the way home, something strange began to happen to Alex. The edges of his body started to shimmer, and he felt hot. "Oh, no," he thought. "I'm getting a cold. And I think I have a fever from standing out in the rain this morning. Just what I need to finish off an already horrible day. Mom and Dad will make me go to bed, and I won't be able to go trick or treating tomorrow night."

Alex looked down. "Am I going crazy?" he gasped. "I can't see my feet." He couldn't see them, but he could feel them. And they felt tingly. He stuck his arms out in front of him. "And I don't have any arms, either. What's happening?"

Alex ran to his house and raced inside. He stood in front of the large mirror in the hallway. He peered into the glass, but nothing was there. "I'm invisible!" Alex cried. He was so shocked, he couldn't move. His heart jumped into his mouth. He had trouble getting his breath. "Calm down," he told himself. Alex stood for a few minutes in front of the mirror, waiting for his breathing to get back to normal.

After a few minutes, he made a bubble. It appeared in the mirror, a pink-and-silver shimmering ball. Alex blew harder, and it grew bigger and bigger. POP, it broke all over Alex's invisible cheeks. He pulled it from his mouth, peeling part of it from his skin, and his face began to appear in the mirror. First his lips, then his nose and eyes, finally his hair and skin. "Oh, boy," he exclaimed, "this gum makes me invisible. When it's in my mouth, I disappear. When I take it out, I become visible again."

Alex took the gum package from his pocket. He squinted at the small black type on the side of the shiny paper. USE AT YOUR OWN RISK. EACH PIECE GOOD FOR TWO HOURS OF CHEWING ONLY. "Wow," Alex thought. "I must be the luckiest kid alive. This gum is magic." He popped the gum back in his mouth and began to feel the hot, tingly sensation he had felt before.

Just then, Pete charged through the front door. He dumped his backpack on a chair and headed for the kitchen. Alex could hear him talking to Nina, their baby-sitter. She worked for the Parsells in the afternoon when Alex and Pete got home from school. She stayed until Mom showed up from work around six.

Alex glanced at his invisible body and a feeling of power surged through his veins. He could do things he'd never done before. He could eavesdrop without being seen. He could steal food from the refrigerator. He could even do a little mischief. He'd start by playing a trick on Pete and Nina.

·2·
THE FLYING PUMPKIN

Alex watched Pete grab a bag of popcorn and a six-pack of Coke from the shelf above the dryer.

"Do you know where Alex is?" asked Nina, flipping the switch on the tape deck. She began humming along to James Taylor.

"Maybe he's at the library," said Pete. "I bet he walked over there after he got off the bus."

Nina shook her head. "He's not supposed to go anywhere without calling. Now I'll just worry until he gets home."

Pete ran to the back door.

"Where are you going?" Nina asked.

"The tree house," said Pete. "The Gang's coming over."

Nina rolled her eyes toward the ceiling. "Please don't bring them in here. I washed the kitchen floor today. But you can take some Fruit Roll-Ups with you. I got them for you and Alex."

"Thanks," said Pete. "Hey, you got strawberry, my favorite flavor."

Nina gave him a friendly pat. "Don't forget your jacket."

"It's too hot for a jacket," said Pete. "My sweatshirt is enough."

Pete dashed outside before Nina could grab his jacket and throw it to him. As she mumbled something about kids and how they never dressed right for playing outdoors, Alex got a Coke for himself. Suddenly Peaches, the Parsellses' golden retriever, sprang up from under the kitchen table. She began to bark. Her body wiggled back and forth. Her tail wagged excitedly.

"What's wrong with you?" asked Nina. Then she saw the Coke hovering in midair. Her hand flew to her mouth. She shut her eyes and rubbed them. "I must be seeing things," she said.

Alex set down the Coke and picked up a pumpkin from the kitchen table. He tossed it in the air, then put it back on the table.

"Help!" cried Nina.

Peaches barked even louder. "You act like you've seen a ghost," Nina said. She touched her head. "For a minute I thought there was one in the kitchen, too." She took Peaches's leash and clamped it to his collar. "I think we need some fresh air," she said. "Let's take a walk."

Peaches kept barking and twisting around to look at Alex. Nina was as pale as the white paint on the kitchen wall. Her skin looked pale against her dark hair.

Alex began to giggle. Then he walked out the door to the tree house, stashing his backpack in the bushes on the way. As he climbed the ladder, he heard voices inside. Rocky and Carlos Lopez were perched on two milk crates near the entrance. Owen Nichols was crouched on the floor with his back to the wall. Pete was balancing on a chair in the middle. Alex sat on a stool in the corner, as far from the others as he could get. Even though he was invisible, he didn't want to get too close to the Gang.

"What should we do for Halloween?" asked Pete.

"Let's take some shaving cream and write HEATHER SMELLS on her front lawn," suggested Rocky.

"That's mean," said Carlos.

"If you're so smart, then you think of something," said Rocky.

Carlos bit his lower lip. "Maybe we could get out our Christmas tree ornaments and decorate the big tree in front of Town Hall."

"That's dumb," said Rocky. "We'd get caught. Mom and Dad would recognize the ornaments."

"How about we soap people's car windows and drape toilet paper on all the trees?" suggested Owen.

"Everyone does that," said Rocky.

"We need to come up with something different," said Pete. "I have an idea that might work."

Alex leaned forward to hear better. The stool fell over, and he landed on the floor. As he frantically tried to get up, Pete said, "How weird. That stool fell over by itself."

"Maybe this tree house is haunted," said Owen.

"I doubt it." Pete shrugged. "Why would a ghost bother to come here? There are too many bigger, spookier places to haunt. Speaking of haunted houses, that's what I want to tell you about. Do you know the old Erdman house? The one on Cleveland Lane?"

"It's not haunted," said Rocky. "It's owned by that creepy old Mrs. Erdman. She lives there by herself."

"She must be a million years old," said Owen. "My mother says Mrs. Erdman lived in that house when Mom was a kid. She's ancient."

"Nina started working for her a few weeks ago," said Pete. "She goes there evenings, after she leaves our house. She stays there until someone else comes to be with the old lady at eleven."

"What kind of work does she do?" asked Owen.

"She gets Mrs. Erdman her dinner. Gets her to sleep. Helps her if she needs anything. She has to stay in bed 'cause she's had a few strokes. Nina says she's always in a bad mood. She orders Nina around and makes her change her sheets and brush her false teeth."

"Wow!" said Rocky. "Does she take her teeth out and put them in a glass every night? Or does Nina brush them when they're still in her mouth?"

"When they're in the glass, dummy. Before the old lady goes to sleep, Nina puts them in a glass on the night table. It's filled with some kind of cleaning fluid. I know, because Nina told me. That's what made me think up my plan."

"So what is your plan?" asked Carlos.

Pete leaned forward, his eyes gleaming. "Let's sneak into the Erdman house and steal the old lady's teeth."

For a moment it was so quiet, you could have heard a penny drop.

"You're crazy," Owen said finally. "Mrs. Erdman would call the police."

"Not if she's asleep," said Pete. "Nina says the old lady goes to bed at eight every night. So we'll go trick or treating after she's asleep. Nina will answer the door with a plate of treats, right? Then Rocky will say he has to go to the bathroom. He'll sneak upstairs and steal the teeth while the rest of us talk to Nina."

"Me?" said Rocky. "Why do I have to steal the teeth? Stealing them is *your* idea."

As the boys argued, goose bumps clung to Alex's skin. Pete's plan sounded good, but risky, too. What if

Mrs. Erdman woke up? And what would the boys do with the teeth once they stole them?

"Okay," said Pete. "I'll do it. But you guys will have to keep Nina busy downstairs. I don't want to get caught."

Alex was worried, but he was excited, too. He could chew another piece of gum and invisibly trail along for fun. The Gang wouldn't know he was there, and he'd be able to watch everything. And be around his brother, too. As Alex fingered the gum that was still in his pocket, he began to feel warm. His fingers started to tingle. The spell must be wearing off!

Alex scrambled toward the entrance of the tree house. He tripped over the ledge and skidded down the ladder. He hit the ground, tingling all over. He saw his running

shoes and jeans, then his jacket and hands grow solid in the gray light of late afternoon.

Alex picked up his backpack and ran around the house to the front door. He knew he'd get a lecture from Nina and later his mother for coming home so late, but he didn't care. All he could think about was the magic gum. Tomorrow at school, he'd chew another piece and have some more fun.

· 3 ·
TWO LIES

Nina was in the kitchen, standing by the door with her arms crossed. Her T-shirt had spots of spaghetti sauce on it.

"Where have you been?" she asked. "I've called the Donaldsens and the Soans, looking for you. Your mother has come home and gone out again to the library, hoping to find you."

"I just came from there," lied Alex. "I was working on my book report."

"Why didn't you come home first? Or call and let me know where you were? I was beginning to think you got kidnapped by the cookie monster." Nina was trying to be serious, but Alex could tell she wasn't too mad.

"I'm sorry," said Alex, looking away from her. "I just didn't think about it." He felt a cramp in his stomach. He wasn't used to lying.

Nina came over and gave him a hug.

"I'm just glad you're back. I sort of missed the sound of your soccer ball bouncing around the kitchen."

Alex groaned. Nina always teased him about using the kitchen floor as a soccer field.

Alex walked to the refrigerator and opened the door. "What's for dinner?"

"Lasagna and salad. And I only used a little meat, since Pete doesn't like it."

Nina went to the back door and opened it. "PEEE-ete," she called.

She took a comb from her purse and ran it through her dark hair. "I wish your mom would hurry up. I have to be at Mrs. Erdman's at six thirty, and I have an exam tomorrow. I need to cram for it tonight."

"What's Mrs. Erdman like?" asked Alex.

Nina shivered. "Old and crabby. That's why I don't want to be late."

The back door flew open and Pete dashed into the kitchen. He unlaced his shoes, threw them under the radiator, and grabbed some crackers from the canister next to the toaster.

"When's dinner?" he asked.

"As soon as your mother gets home," said Nina. "She's at the library, looking for Alex. And don't eat too many crackers. Dinner's good tonight."

"What're we having?"

"Lasagna."

"Yuck," said Pete. "We had it for school lunch today. And why's Mom at the library? Alex is here."

"Duh," said Alex. "Mom doesn't know that."

Pete picked up the pumpkin Alex had held earlier and threw it at his brother.

"Let's carve this while we're waiting," he said.

"Please, not now," said Nina. "It's time to set the table."

"Can't," said Pete. "I've got to call Matthew to get an assignment."

Just then the cordless phone rang. Pete slid across the floor and picked it up.

"It's Mom," he said, cupping his hand over the receiver. Then, taking his hand away, he said, "He's here. Okay. Bye." He hung up and dialed Matthew's number, carrying the phone into the front hall.

Alex got three place mats and some silverware and began setting the table. As Nina put on her hat and jacket, Alex could hear Mom's car pulling into the driveway. The car door banged and her heels clicked up the back walk. She entered the kitchen, her cheeks redder than usual and her eyes flashing. Her normally neat hair was sticking out as if she'd been pulling on it.

"Where have you been?" she asked.

"At the library," said Alex, "working on my book report. You must have arrived right after I left. I'm sorry I didn't call," he finished quickly. He felt another cramp in his stomach.

"Well, all right," said Mom. "But we were very worried. Next time, please remember to let us know where you are."

Alex looked down at the floor. "If she only knew what really happened," he thought.

Nina zipped up her jacket. "I'm going now. The salad's in the fridge and the lasagna's in the microwave. Bye, guys. Don't tear up the house before tomorrow."

"Gee, thanks," said Pete.

"Say hello to Mrs. Erdman for us," said Mom. "And good luck on your exam tomorrow. Come on, kids, let's eat."

During dinner Mom said, "Dad called today. He's stopping at Aunt Meg's for a night while he's in Atlanta. He'll be home on Sunday."

"What time?" asked Pete.

"Late morning," said Mom.

"Good." Pete nodded. "Then he can come watch me play soccer. Our game's at two thirty."

"Can I watch too?" asked Alex.

Pete reached out and punched him gently on the shoulder.

"Sure, Sport, if you promise not to yell at me from the sidelines."

"And could we play a little after the game?" asked Alex.

"We'll see," said Pete. "If there's time, maybe."

But Alex knew there wouldn't be time. The Gang would arrive, and Pete would go off with them. As usual, Alex would be left behind. With Peaches. And Mom and Dad.

· 4 ·
INVISIBLE
IN THE THIRD GRADE

Mrs. DeLarato and some of the room parents had decorated the classroom. Orange and black balloons bobbed along the ceiling. The kids' Halloween poems were stapled to the bulletin board, and the spiders they'd made in art class were dangling from the ceiling. Painted pumpkins lined the windowsill, and a large, black paper cat was taped to the glass pane.

Jane and Umberto's mothers had brought in cupcakes and cider, and everybody had changed into their costumes. They'd already marched in the school parade. Now they were back in their classrooms for their Halloween party.

Alex was dressed as Batman. Mom had ordered the

costume from a catalog, since she wasn't much good at making things from scratch. Last year, she had tried. She'd made Alex dress up as a building that she'd created from a large box. Alex had found it impossible to walk. The kids had made fun of him, and he'd felt like a jerk.

Alex glanced around the room. Isabelle Chubb looked like Dorothy in *The Wizard of Oz*. She had on red high heels and wore her hair in two pigtails. Jason Basso was in a Superman costume. And Ernie Bova was dressed up as Robin Hood. He'd kind of blown it, though. He was wearing a hood that made him look more like some weird kind of monk than like Robin Hood.

Alex didn't like Ernie Bova. Every day on the playground, Ernie called him a wimp and punched him in the face. A couple of times Ernie had tackled him and pushed his face into the sand. The playground aide had stopped him, but Ernie was sneaky. As soon as the aide had gone to another part of the playground, he'd chased Alex again.

Today was Alex's chance to get even.

Mrs. DeLarato clapped. "It's time for the party. We have a special treat today—Mrs. Chubb and Isabelle brought in some pumpkin pies. Isabelle, why don't you help your mom slice them? Here's a plastic knife and some paper plates. The rest of you gather around for the party. Ernie, please help by handing a plate to each person."

As everyone went over to the party table, Alex slipped into the coatroom. Now was the time to get back at Ernie for all the mean things he'd done. Alex pulled his costume down far enough to get a piece of gum from his jeans pocket. He unwrapped it, popped it into his mouth, and waited for the tingling sensation to begin. He felt flushed all over, and within seconds he was invisible.

Alex walked into the classroom. Ernie was leaning over the party table, sniffing one of the pies with his big, ugly nose. "Here goes," Alex thought, running over and pushing Ernie's face into the pie. The pumpkin filling made a squishy sound as Ernie struggled to pull himself free. His face was covered with goo.

"Who did that?" he yelped, swiping at his cheeks with his hands. The class started laughing, all except Isabelle and her mother. They looked angry that one of their pies was ruined.

Mrs. DeLarato was confused. "No one touched you," she said. "You must be imagining things."

Behind the bits of pie plastered to his face, Ernie's skin turned a dark shade of purple. He glowered at the kids who were staring and giggling at him.

"Someone else can help with these dumb pies," he said. Frowning, he went over to Mrs. DeLarato's desk and asked for the pass to the boys' room.

"Ha ha," muttered Alex as Ernie left to get cleaned up. Then Alex scooted invisibly into the hallway. A parade of kindergarteners in costumes was marching down the hall. Alex tugged on the tail of a kid dressed as a cow. The cow turned around and yelled "Quit it!" to the girl behind him. Then he bopped her on the head. She bopped him back.

Alex caught up with the teacher. He whispered "You're cute" in her ear. She jumped. Her Raggedy Ann wig fell over her face.

Alex grinned. Playing tricks was fun.

He walked up the hall to the principal's office. Mrs. Fassbender, the school secretary, was xeroxing some papers at the copying machine. She didn't see the door to Dr. Kazmark's office open. Alex entered and found the principal sitting at his desk, eating a sandwich. He had marched earlier in the Halloween parade, and was dressed as a football player. His shoulder pads made him look twice as big as usual. Alex bent down and grabbed his sandwich. He climbed onto the chair across from the desk. He moved the sandwich back and forth through the air. Dr. Kazmark's eyes bugged out and he leaped up. He tried to get ahold of the sandwich, but Alex moved it just out of reach.

"Oh my gosh," the principal cried. Then he ran out of the room. Alex put the sandwich back on the desk and left the office. Dr. Kazmark was talking to Mrs. Fassbender. "I swear, there's a ghost in this school," he said. "It grabbed my sandwich. I saw my lunch floating around the room."

"There, there," said Mrs. Fassbender. "You've had

a tough week. Let me take you down to the nurse's office."

Alex looked at the clock above the filing cabinets. It was twenty of two. There was less than an hour before the spell would wear off. He'd have just enough time to try a few more tricks. But what if Mrs. DeLarato had noticed he was missing? He decided to go back to the classroom and see what was going on.

· 5 ·
A DOG
IN THE BOYS' ROOM

Alex ran down the third-grade corridor. Luckily no one was around. All the kids were at their room parties. He stuck the gum inside his shoe and waited till he felt hot and tingly. Then, when he could see his body, he slipped into his classroom. The kids were playing pin the legs on the spider.

"There you are, Alex," called his teacher. "Mrs. Chubb was about to go look for you."

"I felt sick," said Alex. "So I went to the bathroom without asking for the pass. I didn't throw up, though. I feel okay now, except that I do have to go to the bathroom. For real."

Alex held his breath. Even though he didn't like to lie, the lie had come easily.

Mrs. DeLarato sighed. Ernie Bova and Jason Basso started to snicker.

"Okay, okay," said the teacher, blindfolding Becca Sciocca and spinning her around. Mrs. DeLarato was so busy trying to keep track of everyone, she didn't seem too concerned about Alex.

Alex took the boys' room pass. When he got to the bathroom, he went into one of the stalls. He unstuck the gum from inside his shoe and popped it into his mouth. Within seconds, he was invisible again. The door opened and a second grader came in to the bathroom. He was dressed as a pirate, with an eye patch and a black hat. His face and hands were covered with sticky orange cupcake frosting. He went to the sink and turned on the water.

Alex remembered how Pete had once locked five dogs in the bathroom at the public library. They had barked like crazy. The librarian had called the police to come get them out. Even though Alex couldn't get ahold of any dogs right now, he could start barking. He opened his mouth and began to howl. Then he imitated Peaches when she yapped at the mailman.

Frantically the second grader looked around.

"Where's the puppy?" he said out loud.

Alex stepped out of the stall and tiptoed over to the

boy. He stuck out his tongue and licked some of the frosting from his face.

"Yuck!" said the second grader. "Who did that?" He wiped Alex's slobber off his cheek. Then he poked his head in the stalls. Seeing nothing, he dashed out of the bathroom without even wiping his hands.

Alex stifled a wave of giggles. As soon as he could control himself, he started barking again. Mr. Fletcher opened the door. He had been Alex's kindergarten teacher. He craned his neck, looking all around, but Alex had stopped barking. Mr. Fletcher withdrew his head. As soon as the door closed, Alex began to bark again. Mr. Fletcher opened the door. Alex shut up. Mr. Fletcher closed the door. Alex started barking again. This went on for a few minutes. Open door. Stop barking. Close door. Start barking. Then Mr. Fletcher disappeared. Alex could hear his steps echoing down the hallway.

"Uh-oh," he thought. "I'd better get back to my class. Mr. Fletcher will be back any minute with a whole bunch of grown-ups."

As if his body could read his mind, it began to grow

hot and tingly. "Anyway, the spell's wearing off," thought Alex as his body came into focus. He sprinted out of the boys' room. Mr. Fletcher and Dr. Kazmark were talking at the end of the hall. Dr. Kazmark looked kind of pale.

"Hi, Alex," he said. "Were you just in the boys' room?"

"Yes," said Alex. He opened his eyes wide, trying to look as innocent as possible.

"Ah ... did you see anything strange in there?" asked Dr. Kazmark.

"Like a dog, perhaps?" asked Mr. Fletcher.

It was all Alex could do to keep from giggling.

"No," he managed to gasp. "What would a dog be doing in the boys' room?"

Then he ran toward homeroom, choking with laughter, before they could ask him any more questions.

·6·
MORE LIES

That afternoon, Mom came into the house with a basket of apples. Alex grabbed one and bit into it.

"Where'd you get these?" he asked.

"I stopped at Terhune's Orchards on the way home. They're for trick-or-treaters tonight."

"MAA-om," said Alex. "No one wants apples."

"Nonsense," said Mom. "Kids need healthy treats as well as candy in their trick-or-treat bags. They'll get plenty of sweets at other houses."

"Mrs. Baumgarten, the school nurse, told us we shouldn't take any apples," said Alex. "They could have razor blades in them."

"Or nails," said Pete.

Mom set the basket on the table. "Honestly, I'm not going to put nails in anybody's apples."

Nina came into the kitchen with Peaches.

"Hello, Nancy. I've marinated the tofu for tonight's dinner," she said. "It's on top of the stove."

"Thanks," said Mom.

"Tofu! Gross!" said Pete. "I hate tofu."

Mom glared at him. "Picky, picky, picky. Maybe you'd like it with ketchup on top."

"No way," said Pete. "Couldn't we have pizza or hot dogs just once?"

Alex watched as Nina undid Peaches's leash and hung it on the hook. "Hey, Nina," he said, "is Mrs. Erdman letting you give out treats tonight?"

"Some fried worms and jellied eyeballs, perhaps," said Nina. "She doesn't like children. Actually, I bought several bags of candy corn. I plan to give out a few treats once she's asleep. If the children aren't too scared to come to her house, that is."

"We'll be there," said Pete. "Me and the Gang are going out right after supper."

Mom tugged nervously on her necklace. "I want you back here by nine. Not one minute later. And no mischief. No tricks. No nonsense. You've been giving me a lot of gray hairs lately."

"How about me?" asked Alex.

"I thought you were going trick or treating with Roshan."

"I am," said Alex, "but when do I have to be back?"

"Nine's all right for you, too. Tonight's a special night. Roshan's dad's still planning to go with you, isn't he?"

Alex had to think quickly. Last night, he had told his mother a lie about Roshan. He had said that he'd been invited to go trick or treating with him, his sister Purna, and their father.

"Yes," said Alex. "He's going with us and dropping

me here when we're all done." Alex swallowed. He hoped this was his last lie.

"Good," said Mom. "Now, I'll finish getting dinner ready while you two start your homework."

Alex looked at his watch. It was five thirty. In three more hours, Mrs. Erdman would be toothless.

· 7 ·
THIEF!

Alex shivered. Even though he was wearing a sweatshirt under his costume, it was cold in the backyard. He'd taken the last three pieces of gum. He'd used one to become invisible a half hour ago. He'd put the second in his pocket. The third he'd hidden in the treasure box on his desk.

Pete was pacing back and forth beneath the tree house. He was wearing a dark cape, and his face was painted white. His lips were red, and he had charcoal marks around his eyes. He looked like Count Dracula.

Owen, Carlos, and Rocky came stamping through the bushes. Rocky was dressed in black and his hair stuck up in spikes. He was probably a rock star or a member of a motorcycle gang. He looked real tough.

It was hard to tell what Carlos was. His skinny arms and legs stuck out around the edges of a handmade shield he'd tied to his chest. It was painted neon orange, and he had antennae on his head that were flashing on and off. He'd painted his face to look like some sort of insect. "Or maybe he's an alien," thought Alex. "He probably made his costume himself. He gets all the art prizes at school."

Owen was wearing his school clothes and parka, but his head was covered by a rubber gorilla mask. With his muscular body, he really did look like a gorilla.

Pete looked at his watch. "Let's do some trick or treating on the way to Mrs. Erdman's. She won't be in bed for another hour."

Alex smiled as he trailed along behind the Gang. Even though he was invisible, he felt sort of like he belonged.

The Gang rang doorbells up and down the streets in the neighborhood. Finally, a little after eight o'clock, they reached the corner of Cleveland Lane. Mrs. Erdman's house loomed above the grass. The shades were drawn in the windows. The tree in front of the house had a KEEP OUT sign on it. At least the porch light was on.

"Give me five," said Pete. The Gang exchanged fives, then opened the gate. Alex's stomach felt fluttery as they trudged up the walk. Leaves blew around their feet. Shutters banged against the side of the house. The wind whistled through the trees.

Nina opened the heavy front door. She came out onto the porch with a big bowl of candy corn.

"Fill your bags," she said. "But be quick about it. I just got old Spider Woman settled."

"Nina," said Pete. "It's us, the Gang."

"My goodness, I didn't recognize you," said Nina. "Your costumes are great."

The boys grabbed fistfuls of candy.

"Hey, Nina," said Pete. "Can I use the bathroom?"

Nina put her finger to her lips.

"I don't know," she whispered. "Old Spider Woman was very touchy tonight. I had to read her an extra chapter of her mystery to get her to sleep. Trick-or-treaters kept ringing the doorbell. I don't want to risk waking her up."

Pete hopped from one foot to the other. "Come on, Nina. I really have to go. I'll be quiet. Very quiet," he continued. "You don't want me to have an accident on the porch, do you?"

Nina jumped back. "I certainly don't. Okay, okay. You can use the bathroom. It's the first door on the right. But be careful. I've heard that vampires lose their power when they pee."

Pete grimaced. Then he went inside. Alex held his breath as he slipped in behind his brother.

The only light in the hallway came from an antique lamp attached to the faded wallpaper. It took a while for Alex's eyes to get used to the dim light. Large moose and elk heads hung from the walls. Their glass eyes glistened mysteriously. A steep stairway stood opposite a cracked mirror.

Alex watched as Pete glanced over his shoulder, then bolted up the stairs. Alex's heart did a few flip-flops. Then he bolted up behind him.

The hallway on the second floor was lined with closed doors. It smelled of ammonia and piano music. Alex broke out in goose bumps as he moved along behind Pete. His brother tried to open the first door, but it was locked. He tiptoed down the hall, then turned into another corridor. At the very end, a door stood slightly ajar. Alex could hear heavy breathing coming from inside the room.

Pete pushed the door all the way open and snuck in. Alex followed, his heart hammering in his chest. An old woman was lying asleep in a big four-poster bed. Her head bobbed against the pale pillows as she gulped in air. Each time she took a breath, her lips quivered. Her skin was as puckered and yellow as old lace. A nerdy-looking kerchief covered her wispy hair. Alex had never seen anyone so old in his whole life.

Pete hardly glanced at her as he approached the night table. Alex held his breath as his brother grabbed the glass with the false teeth. Alex was finally spending time with his older brother, but was it worth it? The anxiety was almost too much. Pete snuck back past the bed and toward the door.

Suddenly there was a loud crash. Pete tripped over a little stool, plunging to his knees and dropping the glass. It fell to the floor and shattered, spilling the cleaning fluid. The teeth clattered sideways under the bed. The old woman's eyes snapped open, two coals burning in her face.

"Nina!" she yelled. "President Clinton! Tom Brokaw! Oh, dear, I am confused. My goodness, there's a thief in my room. And he's after my diamond ring!" She sat up in bed. Her fingers trembled as she pressed a buzzer on the wall. Alex could hear the front door slam as Nina rushed in from the porch. Mrs. Erdman snatched the phone from the bedside table.

Alex stood glued to the floor. He felt like he was watching a dead person come to life.

"Hello? Police? This is Mrs. Edward Erdman at 22 Cleveland Lane. There's a burglary in process...."

Pete had dashed into the hallway. Alex heard him frantically opening and closing doors. Alex knew Pete was in big trouble, especially if something had happened to Mrs. Erdman's diamond ring. Maybe she'd left it in the glass with her false teeth. Any minute, Nina would appear. And so would the police. Suddenly Alex had an idea. For the first time in his life, he realized he could help his brother. If he got him to chew the stick of gum in his pocket, he could rescue him from a fate worse than death.

Alex ran after Pete, opened a door at the end of the hallway, and shoved his brother into a closet. Brooms,

dust mops, and the wand of a vacuum cleaner clattered to the floor.

"It's me, Alex," he said quickly. "There's no time to explain how I got here. I'll tell you later."

As Pete tried to untangle himself, a laundry basket tumbled from a hook above him, clobbering him on the head. Pete waved his arms, trying to get free.

"Where are you?" he finally managed to gasp.

"I'm right next to you. You just can't see me. Here, chew on this piece of gum."

Before Pete knew what was happening, Alex shoved the stick of magic gum into his mouth.

"I feel weird," Pete said after a few seconds. "Like I'm burning up. What's going on?"

"Just chew," ordered Alex.

Nina was running down the hallway. Mrs. Erdman was yelling "Thief! Thief!" from the bedroom. In between yells, she was still talking on the phone. The Gang were probably halfway home by now.

"Lock all the doors," Mrs. Erdman screamed. "In case the burglar is still in the house. And bring me a candlestick. Or better yet, a broom. If he comes back, I want to be ready for him!"

"Or her," cried Nina.

There was more commotion in the hall. Suddenly the door flew open. As the boys faced Nina, holding a candlestick above her head, Pete vanished into thin air.

· 8 ·
CAUGHT!

Nina grabbed a broom and closed the door. "He or she has probably run outside by now," she called.

"I bet it was one of those nasty little trick-or-treaters," yelled Mrs. Erdman. "They almost wore out my doorbell earlier."

"I don't think so," shouted Nina. She was moving up and down the hallway, opening and closing doors. "The kids in this town are nice."

"Not all of them," screeched Mrs. Erdman. "One of Edward's old students fried all our goldfish."

Nina giggled softly but shouted back, "How terrible!"

Alex could hear Nina's footsteps disappearing into

Mrs. Erdman's room. Now was his best chance for helping Pete escape.

He opened the closet door. "Come on," he whispered to his brother.

"When did you get here?" hissed Pete. "And why can't I see you? Why can't I see myself? What's going on?"

"You're invisible," said Alex. "The gum made you invisible. It's magic."

"Wow!" cried Pete.

"Shhh—whisper," ordered Alex. "I'll explain how it works when we get outside."

He pushed his brother toward the stairs. "I can't see you, but I can still touch you."

Alex shoved Pete down the steps. As they ran to the front door, two police cars pulled into the driveway and stopped by the house. Sergeant Musso and another officer sprang from their cars. Alex recognized Sergeant Musso from a school visit. He had given a talk on safety right before Halloween. The sergeant dashed toward the porch. The other policeman turned on a flashlight and ran into the backyard.

Suddenly Alex began to feel tingly and his palms began to sweat.

The spell was wearing off!

He reached underneath his costume and jammed his right hand into his pocket. Then he remembered that the last piece of gum was still in his treasure box at home.

Alex was really hot now. Was it because of what was happening to his body or from nerves? He couldn't tell.

"Pete!" he yelled. "The spell's wearing off. The magic only works for two hours, and my two hours are up!"

"Don't worry," cried Pete. "I'll help you. I'll think of something."

As Sergeant Musso burst through the front door, he found a trembling eight-year-old dressed as Batman cowering in the corner.

· 9 ·
THE GHOST
IN THE BASEMENT

Sergeant Musso grabbed Alex by the arm. "Hey, kid," he said. "We have some serious business to talk about."

Just then Nina came pounding down the stairs, her hair flying out behind her.

"Thank goodness you're here," she said. "I'm Nina Kogan. I work evenings for Mrs. Erdman." Then, seeing Alex, she added, "I think you have the wrong kid." She put her hand to her head and sank into the chair by the umbrella stand.

"What are you talking about?" asked Sergeant Musso.

Buzz, buzz, buzz. Mrs. Erdman was ringing her buzzer. "Bring the police up here," the old lady screamed from upstairs. Even from far away, her voice sounded as shrill as a police siren.

"I'll be there in a minute," yelled Nina. Then, gesturing toward Alex, she said, "I know this kid. And he's not the one."

"Wait a minute," said the sergeant. "Back up and tell me what happened here tonight."

Nina folded and unfolded her hands nervously. Her shirt had come untucked from her pants.

"Whoever went upstairs took a glass from Mrs. Erdman's night table that contained her false teeth and her engagement ring. The burglar tripped and dropped the glass, and the teeth and ring rolled under the bed. I just found them and gave them back to Mrs. Erdman."

Buzz, buzz, buzz. Mrs. Erdman's buzzer was joining the conversation, even if she wasn't.

"How do you know this kid?" asked Sergeant Musso, squeezing Alex's shoulder.

Alex started to feel faint. His hands trembled. Would he be arrested? And where was Pete? He was beginning to hate this night.

"I baby-sit for him after school," said Nina. "It's just a coincidence that he came by to trick or treat while all this was going on."

Buzz, buzz, buzz. Mrs. Erdman was going crazy upstairs.

"Oh, be quiet," hissed Nina.

"So you think it might have been some other trick-or-treater? You just mentioned that this kid is the wrong one."

Nina began to turn red. The events of the evening were catching up with her.

"Well, it could have been his older brother. He was here earlier, along with a few of his friends. He came in to use the bathroom, and right after that Mrs. Erdman woke up and saw someone in her room."

Nina looked at Alex helplessly. She was upset. And probably scared, too. Otherwise, she wouldn't have told.

Sergeant Musso looked down at Alex. "When did you get here?" he asked.

"A few minutes ago," said Alex. Another lie. His stomach did a little somersault.

Sergeant Musso scratched his head. "I'm confused," he said. "If the older brother used the bathroom, where is he now?"

"I don't know," said Nina.

"If you don't get up here soon, I'll call the FBI!" screeched Mrs. Erdman.

"She's something else," said the sergeant. "Is she always like that? I'll question her later. But right now, I want to make sure all the doors are locked. And I need to search the house. Officer Badillo is covering the yard, in case the burglar tries to escape out a window. Where's your basement?"

"Through that door on the left, beyond the stairs," said Nina, pointing down the hallway.

Sergeant Musso let go of Alex's arm. "You wait here, sonny," he said.

Alex plopped down in the chair on the other side of the umbrella stand. His knees were shaking. This was turning into the worst night of his life.

Nina stood up and put her palm on his forehead. "Are you okay?" she asked. Alex nodded, even though he didn't feel okay at all.

"Good," said Nina. "I have to go upstairs and calm down Mrs. Erdman. I'll be back in a minute."

As soon as the two grown-ups had disappeared, Alex breathed a sigh of relief.

"Pete!" he whispered. "What should we do now?"

There was no answer.

"Pete!" said Alex more loudly. "What should I tell Sergeant Musso when he questions me?"

Silence. Had Pete deserted him?

"YOWWWWWWWW! Get me out of here!" Sergeant Musso burst through the door at the end of the hallway and ran past Alex. Alex leaped up.

"There're ghosts in this house," cried the sergeant.

An empty coat attached to a broomstick floated in the air behind the officer.

"Ooooooooo," howled Pete's voice from behind the coat.

Clutching his hat, Sergeant Musso raced outside and jumped into his patrol car. Within seconds, he was backing down the driveway, his siren wailing. He turned onto Cleveland Lane and went speeding to the corner. As he drove toward Stockton Street, he ran over the curb and hit a tree. He backed up, then sped down the street in the other direction.

"Ha ha ha. I sure frightened him," came Pete's voice.

Alex watched the coat float down the hallway and disappear into the basement. A few minutes later, he heard Pete's voice right next to him.

"Come on," Pete said, using his invisible hands to push Alex out the front door. "Let's get out of here before Nina comes back."

Alex darted down the porch steps and flew across the yard. Officer Badillo was turning the corner on the other side of the yard. He was probably wondering what had spooked the sergeant.

"Where'd you get this amazing gum?" Pete asked. He was huffing and puffing beside Alex.

"From the machine at the Mobil station on Mercer Street," said Alex, gulping in air. "It came through the slot when I tried to buy a pack of Double-Bubble Yummy Gum."

"Wow!" gasped Pete. "And the spell only lasts for two hours?"

"Right," said Alex.

"So I'll be invisible for about another hour and a half?"

Alex began to get a prickly feeling at the back of his neck. He didn't like where this conversation was heading.

He slowed down, trying to catch his breath. "Let's stop for a minute," he said.

But there was no answer. Pete was gone.

· 10 ·
A VISIT FROM SERGEANT MUSSO

Mom was waiting by the front door as the church bells struck nine o'clock. She had changed out of her work clothes into her "play clothes"—the jogging pants and bulky sweater she wore when she wanted to feel comfortable. She had also put on a gold mask with glittery beads around the edges.

Alex ran up the steps and into the house.

"Are you all right?" asked Mom. "Where are Roshan and his father?"

Alex was out of breath. He sat down, trying to slow his breathing. He'd have to lie again to keep his mother from finding out what had happened. He was really sick of lying. He took a big breath and looked at the floor.

"They left me at the corner," he said. "Roshan's dad had to get home to make a call. And I ran back here so I wouldn't be late and worry you."

"Oh," said Mom. "Did you have fun?"

"Yes," said Alex. "It was great."

The lies made his stomach cramp up. He wondered if his life would ever get back to normal.

"Where's your trick-or-treat bag?" asked Mom.

"Typical," thought Alex. Mom was a detail person. She noticed everything.

"Roshan's dad has it." He took another deep breath. "I got tired of carrying it around. It was getting heavy. I'll pick it up tomorrow."

Mom looked disappointed. "I was looking forward to a tiny Hershey bar. Or at least a Hershey's Kiss."

"MAA-om. I thought you hated anything with sugar."

"I'm having a relapse. Oh, well, I can always beg a piece of candy off Pete. Where is he, anyway?"

"I haven't seen him," called Alex as he jumped steps to get upstairs. "And I couldn't if I wanted to," he added under his breath. He dove into his room and slammed the door. He wished the door would shut out all the things that were going wrong tonight. He couldn't wait to curl up under his covers. As he started to take off his costume, he heard someone pull into the driveway. He ran to the window and looked out. A patrol car was parking in front of the house.

"Oh, no," thought Alex. "What now?"

A few minutes later, Mom banged on his door. When he didn't open it, she came into his room.

"Sergeant Musso is downstairs," she said. "He wants to ask you a few questions. It seems that both you and Pete were at Mrs. Erdman's house this evening. Someone broke into her room tonight and tried to steal her false teeth and a diamond ring. Do you know anything about this?"

Mom had taken off her mask. Her right eyebrow had climbed to the top of her forehead. Her eyes met Alex's.

Alex looked down at the rug. "I guess I have to talk to him," he mumbled. His feet felt heavy as he followed his mother downstairs. He was really in for it now. Darn that stupid gang. If it weren't for them, he wouldn't be in this mess. Pete and his big ideas.

Sergeant Musso was sitting on the edge of the good couch in the living room. His fleshy face looked soft above his lean body. If he had seen a ghost earlier, he didn't let on.

He cleared his throat.

"Sit down, sonny," he said. Then he took out his notebook.

"I need to get a few things straight about what happened tonight. Did you see your brother or his friends anywhere when you first got to Mrs. Erdman's house?"

Alex hesitated before answering. Should he tell the truth? He didn't see how he could keep lying. But he couldn't tell about the magic gum, either. No one would believe him.

He swallowed. Even though he hated to tell another lie, he decided he had no choice.

"I didn't see any other kids when I got there. I didn't know Pete had arrived earlier and gone inside to use the bathroom until you arrived and Nina told us."

"Was anyone else with you?"

Alex sighed and said, "Roshan, his little sister, and his dad, but they didn't come with me to Mrs. Erdman's. They went trick or treating at the house across the street, and we met up afterward."

Sergeant Musso scribbled furiously in his notebook.

"What are the names of the friends Pete was with?"

"I can answer that," said Mom. She had planted herself behind the chair where Alex was sitting. "Rocky and Carlos Lopez and Owen Nichols."

"I'll need their addresses too, so I can question them. They were on the porch talking to your baby-sitter while the burglar was upstairs. Maybe they know something we don't."

Mom wrote their addresses down on a piece of paper and handed them to the officer.

"If your son Pete shows up, please give me a call," said Sergeant Musso. "I'll keep in touch if I find out anything."

"Thanks," said Mom.

As soon as the sergeant left, Mom started tugging at her hair.

"I hope your brother's not involved in this. But it's strange he hasn't come home yet."

She began to pace the floor. "I could really use a piece of chocolate right now," she said.

Alex longed to tell her about the magic gum, but she'd think he was nuts.

There was only one thing to do, Alex decided. He'd have to find Pete and stop him from getting into any more trouble.

· 11 ·
THE FIGHT

"**I**'m going to bed," Alex told his mother. "If Pete comes back, wake me up, okay?"

"Okay. I'll go call the Lopezes and the Nicholses. I'm hoping the Gang might know where he's gone."

As soon as Mom went into the kitchen to use the phone, Alex slipped out the front door. He jumped on his bike and pedaled toward Stockton Street. He had a hard time biking in a straight line, since smashed pumpkins littered the road.

He took several shortcuts. As he turned the last corner to Stockton Street, he bumped into a drippy paintbrush balancing in midair. A can of red paint was on the pavement in the middle of the street. Next to it was a message spelled out in large letters:

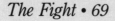

MAVIS PARKER HAS BAD BREATH

"Hey, look where you're going. You almost knocked me over," came Pete's voice out of the darkness.

Alex put on his brakes and dragged his feet on the ground to stop his bike. He wiped a blob of paint from his shoulder.

"Boy, am I glad I found you. Sergeant Musso has been at our house. You'd better get home—fast."

"Not yet. Not until I set off all the fire alarms in town. Then I want to unfasten all the boats in the lake, change the time on the church clock—"

"NO!" cried Alex. "The spell is making you crazy. You have to stop. Mom's really mad. And you're using the gum ... wrong." Alex groped for words. He wasn't sure what he was getting at. All he knew was that being invisible gave you power. And that the power was suddenly becoming... and this was what Alex was struggling with... bad. Dangerous, even.

He grabbed the paintbrush and started painting over the message.

Pete took hold of his arm. "Hey, what do you think you're doing? You're messing everything up."

Alex flung the brush on the grass.

"Okay, okay," said Pete. "I don't care about that dumb message anyway. But I don't want to go home yet."

Pete let go of Alex's arm.

"Uh-oh. My body feels tingly. And I'm awfully hot. I think the spell's wearing off."

Alex glanced at his watch. It was ten twenty.

He breathed a sigh of relief as his brother's black boots, cape, white vest, and the rest of his body appeared next to him. For a second Pete's image shimmered, like the lake water under a full moon. Then he stood, solid and normal, beside Alex.

"What a weird feeling," said Pete. "Now, where did you say you got that gum? At the Mobil station? Let's go see if there's more."

"Forget it," said Alex. "That gum is bad news. And it makes you even nuttier than usual. If you got your hands on more, you'd probably start robbing banks. Or watching the girls in the locker room. We've got to get home. Now!"

"I'll meet you there," said Pete. "I really want to see if there's more magic gum. What did you say it was called? Maybe you should come with me. It's right on the way home. Don't you like to have fun?"

Alex jumped in front of his brother. He grabbed his vest. "Listen. Mrs. Erdman was so upset, she could have had another stroke. And if she blames Nina, Nina could lose her job. Sergeant Musso almost had a heart attack, he was so scared. And Mom is very worried and probably won't sleep all night. Wait until Dad hears about the stolen teeth. I bet he grounds you for a year. So your fun is nothing but trouble for everyone else."

Pete stared at Alex. For a moment, he didn't say anything. He just paced back and forth on the street.

"Okay," he said at last. "Let's make a deal. I'll go home and apologize to Mom and everyone else. But you have to come to the Mobil station first. If there's more gum, we can buy it, but not use it. Not tonight, anyway. We can hide it somewhere and only bring it out if there's a good reason. A long time from now if we need it, I mean."

Alex sighed as he thought about the piece of gum still in his treasure box. He knew he'd have to get rid of it when they got home. He wished that all the gum in the machine were gone. But maybe it was. Maybe the pack he'd bought had been some kind of fluke. He thought about Pete's offer. He decided to go along with it. It was his best chance at getting Pete home. He just hoped the gum machine would be empty.

· 12 ·
THE GUM MACHINE

At the Mobil station, Alex hopped from foot to foot as Pete stared at the machine.

"Tell me again, how did you get the magic gum?" he asked.

"I put in the coins and pushed the buttons for Double-Bubble Yummy Gum, and a package of ZXO's Double-Trouble Bubble Gum came out instead."

"Let's try it," said Pete. He fiddled in his pocket for some change. Then he plunked seventy-five cents into the coin slot and pushed the buttons for Double-Bubble Yummy Gum.

The boys leaned down, their noses almost touching the tray, as the gum dropped into the opening.

74

Pete reached in, grabbed it, and read the label.

"Darn!" he said. "It's normal. You try. Maybe it takes your magic touch." He shoved some coins into Alex's hand.

Alex hesitated, then poked them into the slot and pushed the buttons for the code. Somehow he knew, as sure as he'd ever known anything, that ZXO's Double-

Trouble Bubble Gum was a thing of the past. Another pack of Double-Bubble Yummy Gum dropped into the tray.

"Come on," he said. "There isn't any more."

"Too bad," said Pete. "It would have come in handy for copying off people's homework."

Alex shook his head. Wouldn't his brother ever learn? Well, maybe Pete had learned something. Alex sure had. He knew now that he didn't want anything more to do with the Gang. His brother could hang out with them all he wanted, but Alex was going back to his old life.

Pete put his arm around Alex's shoulders.

"Let's go, little brother," he said. "Climb on the handlebars. I'll give you a ride home. And tomorrow, we can play some soccer."

· 13 ·
A WOOF
IN THE BATHROOM

Mom was sitting in the living room watching TV. A cup of coffee was on the table beside her. She leaped up when Alex and Pete walked in.

"Thank goodness," she said. "Where have you been? And Alex, why aren't you up in bed?"

"I was worried about Pete," said Alex, "so I snuck out to look for him. I found him in the tree house."

Alex hoped this was the last lie he'd ever have to tell.

"Great," said Mom, tugging at her hair. "Now I have two of you I have to worry about." She went over to the table and poured herself another cup of coffee. "I don't know if I should hug you or kill you." Then she hugged both of them. "Okay," she said, "I want the whole story. No omissions. No lies. Only the truth."

Alex looked over at Pete. He was as white as a marsh-mallow.

"I'm sorry," said Pete. "I didn't mean to cause so much trouble. I was just trying to have a little fun on Halloween. I guess I went too far. I planned to steal the teeth, but I had no idea there was also a diamond ring in the glass. I dropped everything, and then Mrs. Erdman woke up and called the police. I got away before they could arrest me." Pete glanced at Alex, a tiny smile tugging at the corners of his mouth. "I was hiding in the tree house when Alex found me."

Alex smiled back. He knew that the invisible gum would be their secret. Forever. That almost made the whole evening worth it.

"I'm going to call Sergeant Musso," said Mom. "If you're able to convince him you didn't mean any harm, he'll probably only give you a warning. After all, you never left the house with the stolen goods. And you didn't break and enter, since Nina let you in. As for you, Alex, I'm disappointed that you left the house to look for Pete without asking. But I'm also glad that you found him. You should both go to bed. I'll phone your father, and tomorrow I'll let you know what we've decided to do about all this." Then she smiled. "Pete, could you throw me a chocolate from your trick-or-treat bag?"

"Gosh, Mom," said Pete, "I don't want you to die from a sugar overdose." Then he gave her a candy Kiss and a real kiss.

Alex couldn't get upstairs fast enough. Before putting on his pajamas, he ran over to his treasure box and lifted out the last piece of gum.

He carried it into the bathroom. He stood over the toilet bowl. Could he really do this? He thought about the good times he'd had being invisible in school. And the bad times he'd had that night with Pete. Well, maybe not all bad. Something between them had changed. They would be seeing more of each other. Hadn't Pete promised to play soccer with him tomorrow? Still, the magic gum did lead to "double trouble," just like the label said. Alex took a deep breath. Then he dropped the gum in the water. The packet glowed mysteriously as it hit the surface with a small sizzling noise.

Alex flushed the toilet, and the water gurgled as it swished around the bowl.

Just then, Peaches padded into the bathroom and shoved her head into the water to get a long, cool drink.

Alex was so surprised that for a minute he didn't realize what was happening.

His eyes bugged out as he looked down and saw his dog lapping up the magic gum. She began to whimper and pant as her nose grew wet and drippy. Within seconds, she had disappeared.

Alex put his hands to his head. A loud woof filled the bathroom.

Then, opening the door, Alex scurried to his bedroom and dove under the covers. He pulled the pillow over his head to drown out the barking that was now coming from the hall.

This, he decided, was a Halloween that he would never, ever forget.